READING LEVEL
3C

MW00929766

THE FOREST OF THE FUTURE

AUTHOR:
Margaret Muthee

ILLUSTRATOR:
Bruno Iradukunda

CREATIVE DIRECTOR & EDITOR:
Michael Ross

CONTENT ADVISOR & EDITOR:
Hilary Rogers

TRANSLATIONS BY:
Margaret Muthee , Beryl Oywer

nabu.org
110 East 25th Street,
New York, NY 10010

Chris and Kwanza are cousins. They are best friends, and even though they've never met in person they chat online every single week.

They tell each other everything. All the good things that happen, and all the bad things that happen. Most of all, they share a strong interest in climate change.

Chris and Kwanza live on opposite sides of the world. Chris lives in New York, the city of lights, colour, excitement and laughter.

Kwanza lives in Ukunda, a small town on the south coast of Mombasa. She lives by the shore and loves listening to the dancing waves of the ocean at night.

Chris tells Kwanza about the beautiful buildings and loud sounds of New York. But he has always grown up with concrete beneath his feet, and some days he can hardly see the sky between the high buildings.

Kwanza explains about life in her small town. She lives close to the Kaya Ukunda forest. It was once beautiful, green, and home to all sorts of animals. But much of the forest has been cut down. Only a few of her favorite trees remain.

Sometimes Chris feels sad that he has never seen the forests of Kenya. He wants to meet his extended family, and be surrounded by people who look just like him.

Sometimes Kwanza wishes she could see the buildings and museums of America. She wonders if she is missing out on all the cool things her cousin is experiencing.

Both Chris and Kwanza count the days until Chris turns 10. Of course, 10 is a great age to be. But more than that, it's when Chris and his family are visiting Kenya! Chris has been saving his pocket money all year.

Before long, Chris watches the tall buildings become dots on the earth. He wonders what he'll find on the other side. The clouds soon cover everything up.

At first he and Kwanza feel shy to one another. There
has always been so much screen between them. But
soon their shyness fades, and they are inseparable.

Kwanza shows Chris her town. It's buzzing with exciting sounds of hooting matatus, and friendly smiles from the people. Chris takes in everything. He feels a warmth growing in his heart.

They see where the beautiful forest used to be. Now it is dry, barren earth. There is no wildlife, no shade, no wonderful forest smells. Chris and Kwanza decide to take action.

They will plant 200 trees a day for one week.
Soon other children from the village hear
about their plan and join in.

It's sweaty. It's hard work.
But it feels so wonderful to have a plan and act on it!

Once the children planting is finished, the elders perform a ceremony to bless the trees. They sprinkle water with their whisks and lead the villagers in chanting and dancing. Kwanza and Chris decide to call it **The Forest of The Future.**

The children head to Kwanza's house with tired muscles and happy hearts. They joke that there is now magic in the ground, and when they return tomorrow, the forest will be lush and fully grown.

They share a delicious meal and drift into a gentle sleep beneath the twinkling stars. Chris never wants to leave.

In the morning, after a bowl of ugali, the children run to their newly planted forest.

They cannot believe their eyes. Glorious native trees
tower above them like great green buildings. Birds fly
from branch to branch and small animals
scurry in the undergrowth.

"How is this possible?" Chris asks.
"It's magic! The spirit of the forest is alive,"
Kwanza whispers in awe.

The entire forest has regrown overnight. The children breathe in the sweet forest smells. Never have they felt more alive and positive about the future !

They spend the last days before Chris needs to go back
enjoying the forest with the entire village and everyone
who helped them.

Saying goodbye is sad, but already they are saving their pocket money so Kwanza can visit Chris in America.

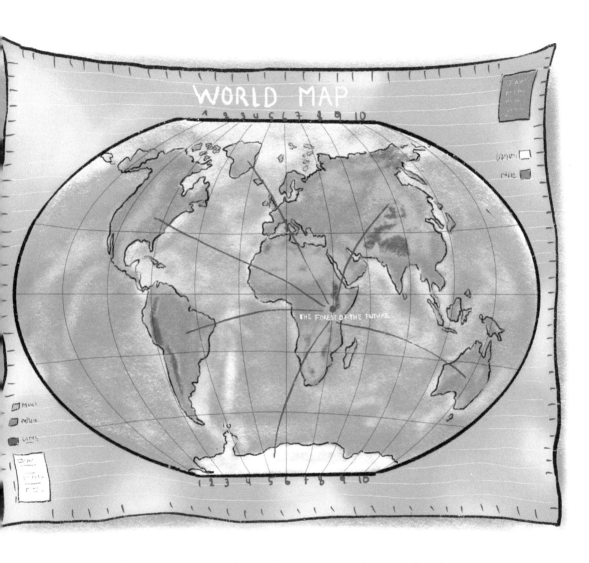

The only question is, where to plant their next forest of the future?

The Forest of the Future

NABU

nabu.org

110 East 25th Street,
New York, NY 10010

CPSIA information can be obtained
at www.ICGtesting.com
Printed in the USA
BVHW021954150221
600189BV00004B/19